Bianca and Jezebel
Edward Holman II

Bianca and Jezebel

Edward Holman II

E. Holman II - a Wolf Publisher®™

Portland, Oregon, USA 97266

®™Rated: Y A – Young Adult 16+

Over 16 Highly Recommended

®™M A – Mature Audiences

God Bless you all; and enjoy this make-believe world, one

in which I would not wish to live in myself, under any

circumstances nor should anyone else. Stay safe and mindful.

Ed

Dedication

Dedicated to my sister Letha, and my 5 kids, Eddie III, Michael, Kevin, Christopher, and Jennifer… without them I'd be lost and all alone in this world.

To all of the great authors Poe, King, Spielberg, Sterling, Shakespeare, Brothers Grimm, Carroll, Dickens, Aesop, Hans Christian Andersen, Victor Hugo, Mark Twain, and so many more, not to forget those in the here and now who have given me so much inspiration that it haunts me to know their spirits still flourishes deep inside of my wondering existence that lay with-in this delicate and unknown world of the all-seeing mind's eye.

My spirit is filled with sincere and humble gratitude for all here who helped me in my novel achievement and who encouraged me throughout my writing career.

I thank you sincerely.

Edward Holman II

Preface

Inside a chaotic life style where misery seems to love company; when conflicts arise between siblings who are exact duplicates of one another, but different inside their demeanors; and, when blood is drawn and exchanged between them to the point of causing a body swap, these two rough and tumble kids have nowhere to run or hide with an evil witch tormenting and causing all the more confusion than they have already displayed to their mother, and everyone around them; they are unable to escape a fate worse than death because bad things will happen when you try to run away from your problems… So beware of all that life throws in your face!!! Beware. Go figure!

Bianca and Jezebel

Not so once upon a time there was a beautiful young woman who' husband just up and left her all alone in a cottage deep in the woods to fend for herself and her two identical twin girls. Her garden used to have beautiful roses growing from a tall tree all year long, one with white and one with the oddest black roses none like anyone had seen the likes of before.

Now it so happened, that her two children, one named Bianca Snowella Rose and the other had the dismal name of Jezebel Briaretta Rose. They were like day and night, always bickering and fighting when together. Snowella was not so gentle most of the time when alone or around others, but Briaretta, she was like an angel, always helpful and friendly to everyone.

Nowadays you would think that with the names they had that it would be the opposite of their own characters, but that was far from the case in every insane instance set before them, their mother, and all of us.

Jezebel be fond of all the goody-two shoes stuff of the kind mentioned; such as, always helping her mother around the cottage, cooking, cleaning, sowing, and reading dreamy stories to her illiterate mom with happy endings when her sister was wondering about the countryside, and that pleased her mom very much.

Snowella liked causing havoc everywhere she went, always picking on everyone especially the good little boys and girls who lived in and near Un-Enchanted Ville here in the Oregon wilderness, a small town adjoining the bottom of the gorge where the trout live in a dale filled with antiquity and a seamless, no end laced skirted lifestyle.

As I know, the two girls weren't very fond of one another; always taking to - push come shove with lots of hair pulling and often bloody noses, or some other sort of blood-spattered injury, and neither one trusted the other in the least.

Their mother overheard them bickering one afternoon and confronted them sternly, but with keeping her calm and dignity intact.

"Jezzy you make me sick to my stomach and I so often wish that I was the only one and you were dead." Bianca said with such a sneer on her pickle puss face.

"Likewise to you my little black roses witch sister, I am so sorry to say, but without regret." Said Etta. That's what she sometimes liked to be called by her closes friends as well as even some adults including her mother at times.

"Girls – girls, now you need to stop all of this fighting and arguing all the time… my goodness your both such a mess, straight away get behind the house and clean yourselves up pronto do you hear me, I will be watching you both and if I see or hear anything at all I will have to tan your hides. Is that clear?" Their mother said in a somewhat gentle tone with meaning behind her words, but they both knew their mother wouldn't spank their backsides in the least.

"Yes Mother." They both said at the same time staring each other in the eyeballs with pure evil blows of the other kind, and if looks would kill, well then it would ultimately happen in half a shake of a wolf's tail.

While their mother was busy preparing their supper; the two girls had a spat over the pump as to who went first; and as it happened, Snow pushed Jezzy down in a mud puddle getting her dress a royal brown mess. Well, if the pumps fit, Jezzy scurried to slip her way back into an upright position; she took off after her mean sister as fast as a rabbit towards the big rose tree and all those lovely thorns; the scuffle was on, and smack dab into them they flew tearing both girls dresses to threads along with cutting them to pieces leaving several thorns in each other's hands and legs.

"Owuie, ouchy, yawza. Damn you Jezzy. You'll get yern one day girly boo." Said Bianca.

"Not if I – ouchy, witch, get you first. Damn that hurts. Momma, momma, come see what batty bratty done did to me." Cried Jezebel.

Well; in most cases, the woods was a good place to live if you were bear, rabbit, or squirrel or whatever; and, none of the animals bothered any of the humans, but on occasions such as this one they'd get curious enough to poke themselves from their hiding places just to see what was disturbing their peace and quiet. Outside of some of the local birds cheerfully- chirping a meadow melody off in the distance now and then, all was not quite as it usually was, but chaotic instead.

At times one or two of the little hare would eat a small leaf of cabbage or carrot out of Jezebel's hand and then scurry away with a nice chunk of it in its bucktoothed little mouth to feed its family that lived in a nearby bunch of bushes next to a hallowed out rotten tree, while a stag would leap merrily by as birds looked onward with curiosity as well.

The two had gotten even messier than they had been from earlier, and that was sure not to please their mother in the least. They knew that if they didn't get back to the pump and clean up that their punishment would be a tad harsh, so they abandoned their fight and dashed themselves back to the pump before they got in even deeper trouble.

In the process of their fight, they'd exchanged blood with each other, but were unaware that anything was wrong, so they got undressed and washed themselves up like they'd been told to; luckily for them they didn't get found out and was safe this time, but next time they may not be so blessed.

After they ate their supper, they went to bed hurting so bad that tears wouldn't come, more-so for Bianca Snowella, so she decided to sneak out of the cottage and spend the night in the woods away from her tamed and somewhat ugly sister, at least in her mind's eye anyhow; and, as dawn began to peak its head through the tree branches, a beautiful little girl in a brightly lit colorless dress stood beside her where she lay; startling her to a complete awakening of a different kind than she'd most often been used too.

The little girl peered quite kindly at her, but Snowy gave her the usual wicked evil eye and a sneering hiss as to ask; "Who the pooh are you, and what are you doing bothering me anyway?" Sniffled Bianca still a tad bit teary eyed over the brawl she'd had with her sister Jezebel.

She said nothing and went quietly back into the forest whence she came and disappeared as if she'd never even been there in the first place.

Bianca glanced and seen that she had laid herself down too close to a very dangerously high cliff and may have very well fallen into its deepest dark secret if she'd been a few inches closer to its edge. Perhaps, the edge of night, if I may be bold and beautiful enough to say it in mere thoughts to such nonsense and falsehood to what all soapy things as they, may present to you.

Snowy rushed herself back home and climbed back into her bedroom window so she wouldn't get caught, but when she looked, her sister Jezebel wasn't there; and she thought that she'd already awakened, had ate her breakfast, and subsequently went on out to make more trouble for the town of Un-Enchanted Ville as she usually done on a Saturday morning before daylight made it too hot for her in more than one way.

"Good morning mother." Bianca said in a very usually gleeful voice.

"Good morning Bianca. My-my, you're up mighty early today; how's my little Etta?" She seemed a bit confused now and then since the girls were identical twins, but was in a rather chirping mood to some extent since she'd gotten plenty of rest after a bit of a stressful Friday.

"I'm Jezebel mother; don't you know us by now, anyway mommy, where's my mean sister Snowy-flake- the wicked witch of our wonderful Canyon community?" Since the scuffle she had with the real Jezebel yesterday, and the thorn incident; Bianca had become Jezebel and vice versa, and her attitude seemed to have changed in some bizarre and abnormal way, her attitude was beginning to be good and she was acting and sounding just like her sister Jezebel instead of the mean little girl she had always been.

"Why Bianca, or Jezebel I mean, that don't sound a bit like you my darling, I know your upset over the fight you had with your sister yesterday, but please calm down and be your usual pleasant self, all righty?" She was shocked at how her good little girl was acting and went on about her business as usual.

"Well, mother, she is such a menace, you know that don't you?" Bianca said in a snobbish tone, but then apologized immediately with a tear in her bright sky-blue eyes.

"I'm sorry mother, I don't know what come over me; I guess it was the fight we had." She said taking her dress sleeve and wiping her nose and then her eyes on it just like Jezebel always done. Old habits are hard to break as a girl gets older and changes in attitude as her puberty leaves; and the teenage stage of thirteen begins.

"Is there something else wrong this morning that you'd like to talk to me about?" The Lady Fanny Charmed Rose asked of her daughter with a curious brow raised expression on her way too early mid-life crises face.

"Not really mommy dearest; it's just that I went out last night and had fallen asleep by a steep ledge and came back this morning before dawn, but the strangest thing happened to me while I was there." She seemed puzzled, and continued as her mom looked onward all the more curious. "Well, anyhow a strange little girl in a shiny ashen dress was standing beside me when I awakened and frightened me and then she went off into the woods out of site without saying a single word; but oh well, nothing happened. I'm hungry, let's eat so I can go play – okie-dokie, please mommy dearest." She bellowed, save for sounding odd to her mother who pondered over her words and actions as she made their breakfast.

"I haven't seen your sister Bianca since last night; she may just be playing with her forest friends. What happened to you in the forest; that must have been an angel looking out for you to let you know you could have fallen over that cliff and had something terrible happen to you… now don't you go doing something so dangerous like that again, do you hear me Bianca; I mean Jezebel. Dad nab it, you two, have always made me as if Confucius, but you know sweetie pie, I need your help; I do love you so, sit here and let's eat? Abeg, be careful from now on. Geesh. Children." Her mother said in a stern; but mellow pitch.

More often than not; Bianca helped keep the cottage so clean and neat so that those who came to visit periodically were well pleased to look inside in addition to chit chatting the day away with the lonely Ms. Fanny Charmed Rose while the children were out playing. It was out of habit that Bianca kept up with things like a good little teeny-bopper girl would do; this day wasn't the normal one of which little Etta didn't want to take under her wings; she didn't do any cleaning after breakfast, and never picked any of the beautiful flowers to place in a vase full of clear spring water to put on the center of the dining room table to make it a thing of sheer beauty along with having the air full of rosy perfume like the whole outside, but after she ate, the real Bianca who was becoming her sister Jezebel took off out the door like a bat out of Hades. Her mom didn't get a single word out edgewise in any way, form, or shape… creating such a puzzle before her big late springy sky-blue eyes.

Soon winter had befallen upon them. It was unusual to have white flakes coming down upon their community; sort of a welcome sight, but the cold was horrendous, with a southern wind speeding through the canyon, over the big river and through the woods like an olden times train just to get to the end of the line in order to allow still more of the same to follow close behind. It oozed its way along the Sandy water ways every twist and usually mellow turns, but this time seemed a bit different, yet no one had any idea as to what was really going on here in the other la-la land high above the Californication state of druggies, crossdressers and gangland thugs, and the likes.

All of the kettles had been polished and shining like golden flakes sparkling above the fireplace that was roaring to the slight of breeze that drifted down the chimney to keep it going strong enough to create the much-needed warmth for all concerned.

When evening come about the cottage, Fanny bolted the door so it wouldn't blow open chaotically; and then, sat herself down with a good book of fairytales next to the nice cozy fire that had an extended hearth what would also be heated to make all the more of a temperate climate to settle down into?

She got so into her book that the thought of her two daughters never entered into her mind's eye in the least. After she finished one of the stories inside her wonderful hardback; Fanny headed off to bed thinking the two girls were already in their bed all snug as a bug in a rug, and fell fast asleep, right there in her easy-girly rocking chair.

Her head was filled with visions of sugar plumbs dancing about like little lambs, with two white doves hovering above her and them. The wind blew furiously flapping the screen door that she's forgot to latch as well and was awakened as if someone was knocking on her little hell hole in the woods tree cottage.

Well, she thought that it may have been a wayward traveler seeking shelter from the in climate and unusual weather they were having in the canyon; when she peered out a nearby window by the door, no one was there; her eyes still not quite open, seen that it was just the screen banging to and fro against its counterpart, but she just ignored it and went to her nice comfy bed; back aching, covering up her head to the cold world around her – she fell fast asleep once again.

Meanwhile out in the woods, Jezebel the newly transformed Bianca had gotten herself lost as had the real Bianca what was now Jezebel who usually knew where she was at all times, but this time she had not one clue where the blue ball blazes she was. Well; as it so happened, Jezzy talked to all of the animals and sometimes they seemed as if they were talking back to her.

"Don't be troubled my friend, I will do you no harm." Said a wayward black bear that had come across the lost Jezebel-Bianca Rose.

"Oh, I am not afraid of any of you animals in the least. T-hehe-t-he." Jezzy said with a smile and giggle.

But the bear said the weirdest thing to her after a moment of silence.

"I know who you really are and what happened to you a couple days ago; you had a fight with your sister and took on her blood and she yours after you pulled on each other in the thorns of the big rose tree." He spoke in a deep baritone voice that clattered inside Bianca's head like a rattlesnake shaking its tail in warning to back off and not be so close to her face.

"I am not who you say I am, I am me, I am Jezebel Briaretta Rose the good girl and not that mean sister of mine Bianca Snowella Rose, am I not? She seemed confused and shook her head and had caused the bear to stand herself down on all fours and bounced heavily away back out into the forest whence it had come.

Now we all know that animals can't really talk, but at times it sure seems that way; and well, Bianca was confused all the more and believed her conversation with that bear really took place and she too ran deeper in to the forest and got all the more lost than she already was.

Bianca was half frozen from snow, wind and the cold; and so wished that she was back at home by the nice warm fire

with her mother and her sister in spite of not getting along with
the real Jezebel the real goody two shoes or her mother as far
as that went at times as well.

She began to cry immensely creating tiny drops of icicles
below her cloudy and misty eyes; and on her glowing puffed
out red cheeks; she give the impression of being a Christmas
tree all pastel on top of her forcefully temperamental and dark
interior without any presents under her shivering branches.

Briaretta Snowella didn't know what to do let alone knowing
where to go and in what direction as another evening was
upon her; so she followed the moss what was always on the
north side not to allow her southern exposure to show as the
wind began to pick up her nightgowns tail.

Soon she came upon a cave; Jezebel was nearly frozen
like a Popsicle as she went on in not knowing if it was a
dangerous place or not? As she walked slowly inward, her
body began to get warmer and her early winter thaw began to
come forth as if she were at home by the fireside.

Much to her surprise she looked and there all curled up in one corner of the cave was a bear with its two cubs and it scared her near to the point of no return; forcing herself to walk backwards instead of forward to gain the body heat from the bears to help unthaw herself with in hopes the bear would not awaken and eat her alive.

All the sudden she stumbled and almost landed in some baby bear droppings when she tripped once again on a different rock and landed on her skinny behind; up went her dress over her head like her blanket at home that seemed to be always covering her not so cute teenaged face showing a few zits. Yes. Even dark-skinned chicks get them. Don't you know.

"Yew, yuck-o! Crapola." She said, letting out a slight screech when her hand toughed the bear pooh; her unintentional scream awoke all the bears in the cave; well as it was in the animal kingdom; they got curious enough to get up from their hibernation to see what the noise was. As they came near to Bianca and sniffed her butt, she shuffled herself backwards as fast as her hands and legs could take her in such an out of shape position throwing her dress back down over her legs, she looked straight into the eyes of that big bears glowing brown eyes and couldn't scream one more iota of a note if her life depended upon it; which it ultimately did, but the bears just looked at her and then turned back around and headed back to their bed since they had already chowed down their bellies full enough to take them clean through to the next spring thaw.

Bianca couldn't believe her eyes and went to a different spot and curled herself up into her own little ball and also fell fast asleep.

When dawn awoke; so did Bianca, but she wasn't afraid of the bears because they were too far gone into their hibernation to hinder any of her sudden movements as long as she didn't scream or anything like that again, she knew that she'd be alright, but she was so hungry that almost anything looked good enough to eat, so she snuck outside to scavenge the forest for things she knew was consumable enough for humans as well as animals, and since they too for the most part were such picky eaters, she felt it a good thing also for her own survival.

Once she found some late fallen hickory nuts that hadn't yet gone bad with some bear tracks beside them, she knew that they'd be a fairly good start on curing her angry belly that was growling like one of them big old bears in the cave.

As she continued to search for other wild things good enough to eat, she found some human foot prints in the snow; and low and behold, they matched her own foot prints. Well her head began to bubble with joy and excitement that she'd be able to find her way back home as long as the foot prints lasted; all would be fine and dandy in no time at all if her luck held out.

Bianca felt a whole lot more comfortable, but still, she was not all that content thinking constantly about, what if this, what if that, what would happen next, then she'd be so lost and all alone in the world, but she had to maintain her sanity enough not to give up so easily. She tried to think like her sister did, but it seemed to be an extremely hardened taffy candy task to chew on as she walked still following the foot prints that hadn't melted away yet.

Just around the bend she came upon a make shift shelter constructed out of lots of fallen tree branches and other scavenged objects and said in an outcry; "Hello, is anyone here, please help me, I'm lost and can't find my way back home; please anyone, someone please help me." Her voice flew through the forest, but there wasn't any answer and she began to cry once again. Quickly she dried her eyes so they wouldn't turn back into tiny icicles and crimson her already puffy and weather parched skin all the more followed by pain every time she chafe them with such an irritation that it made her all the more afraid, but to top that off she began to become annoyed and angry bothering her all the more. Her patience was running out making it even harder to get a grip on her senses.

It seemed like it was getting late once again, and since there was a shelter of sort, Bianca, uhm, Jezebel thought to herself; "Well, no one answered me back, I'm just going to claim this for my own little weather beater and get me a much needed nap or maybe even stay the night." It was better than nothing at all and the cold came upon her once more as she done her best to cover herself up with some of the old rags and such that lay inside the lean-to, and wowy-wow-wowzers did it feel so good to her bones and chilly black roses flesh.

As Bianca lay there; her thoughts kept heading home where her mother and sister was; sitting by the fire and warm hearth all safe and cozy from the cold and bad weather that had hit the region a tad earlier than usual; snow was something she was use too but not this early, nor its blast chiller kind anyhow.

Time gave the impression to stand as still as the night sky, and it was hard for her to fall asleep in such a make-shift outside haphazard shelter as she lay in, but it would have to do until she either made her way back home where she'd be safe or found a much better place hopefully with human inhabitants actually occupying it that wouldn't harm her or think her the bad girl she really use to be.

The night flew by faster than one could imagine, and Bianca the for real Jezebel awoke at the butt crack of dawn and began once more trotting through the forest all white and frosty. The foot prints seemed to be getting less and less as she walked and still no sign of any human beings for her to get close enough to so she could chit chat with them as to where she was, and about how to get back home where she really belonged. As she walked, her darkness began to turn ghost-like, and that really made her all the more uncomfortable to her new surroundings.

Soon she came across still another cave which struck her odd; it looked mighty familiar but she thought it was a totally new one, so she went inside just like she did the first one, and much to her surprise; there was three bears in it just like the other cave. She shook her head and shed a couple tears as she realized that she had went in a big circle and hadn't gained any real distance between the forest she was lost in and her home; not one speck had she accomplished her objective to regain what she had taken away from her at her own expense of running away in the first place.

Bianca set herself down on the rock that she'd tripped over the day before pondering over what to do next; she thought and thought and decided to spend still that night in the cave once again since the bears were still fool-heartedly steadfast asleep for the duration of the winter months; and then, she'd head out bright and early the next morning in the opposite direction and hopefully she'd come across someone sooner or later, hopefully much sooner than the latter.

Once more the night passed itself away faster than a frightened rabbit and she headed out again.

Bianca-Jezebel walked and walked and finally she came upon a cottage that she thought was her home, but when she went inside, she was not only shocked at what she saw, but startled the people what lived inside as well.

"Oh, I'm sorry… I'm lost and thought this was my home, please forgive me for intruding, but please can you help me, I been wondering through the forest for several days if not a week or more… I don't know where I am and I'm cold and hungry too." She began to cry but once again she quickly wiped her tears from her eyes and runny nose upon her dress sleeve. The warmth from the fire was a welcome sight as was the smell of some much needed and delicious food.

A woman walked over to her and introduced herself as Wanda Wolf, and threw her arm around Snowella's waist and escorted her to the table and sat her down; then quickly asked one of the other tiny girls to get her a plate of hot deer stew and a nice hot cup of chickaree with goat milk and honey in it.

"Here dearie, this will help make you feel much better; please eat." She smiled as big as the full moon and sat down beside her.

But before she said another word, Snowy had finished the whole plate and gave a sigh of relief as she took another big gulp of the hot brewed chickaree and gave another sigh of relief.

"My-me, madame Wanda, that was good… thank you so very much, but please can you tell me where I am and how to get home; I miss my momma and even my mean twin sister who I am always having fights with?" She asked in a somewhat rude way, but also a pleasant squelch as if she'd been walking on muddled ground for her entire life of giving way to such rude pitch out of her chapped and cracked lips.

"Slow down child." Said the woman as her six children; all girls, just giggled and went on about their business as usual, and then the woman continued to speak. "I am the Mother of the Forest, Wanda, and these are my children. My husband, God rest his soul passed some years back leaving me baron, but the creator gave me these six wonderful little girls to raise all by myself; we do well, and the town of Nowhere Ville lay a couple miles from my cottage." She could talk on and on if given half a chance to, but Bianca Snowy interrupted her once more.

"But-but how do I get home, I have never been here in all my life, but my mean sister may have been here way too many times causing all sorts of problems, do you know of her; have you seen her; I want her to take me home, please tell me?” Bianca said with many questions in her mind, but took to stillness with a crushing retort instead of listening to the old woman’s muddling rambling on’ so she could get an answer to her questions.

There seemed to be a put the lid on censor to her newly acquired surroundings as all the children gathered round Bianca the now totally transformed good girl Jezebel Briaretta Rose.

“Children; come now children, take her to one of our many rooms and fit her with some new and dry clothing to make her all the more comfy; quickly now, time is paramount. Bianca’s essence will be more than willing to stay like all of you have already done so to be all of my children for eternity; it is essential for all of you to make it her purity secondary to nature so that she will identify herself as being one of our family and let her past go. It will be nightfall once again soon; heavier snow will come down upon us all and we won’t be able to get out for several more months until the next spring sets its sight on Nowhere Ville and all of us. My-my how my family keeps growing faster than I'd like sometimes, but that's how it is supposed to be since I am the mother of the lost forest." Mother Nature demanded of the lost realm of Un-Enchanted Ville here inside her mental state of the Oregon wilderness adjacent in proximity to the lands of port Multnomah water brouhaha and the valley of wine and roses.

If it was out of sheer convenience to the remoteness in an outlying relationship that had taken place in the proximity that lead space and time through the corridor of which Bianca got herself lost and come upon the cottage of the mother nature of the lost way back in not so once upon a time; to the propinquity of becoming blood relations to Mother Nature and all of the other lost little girls, then the green grasses of spring may have not even came to the pilferage form of Jezebel's insight as to the lost forest of the Great Pacific Northwest in the first place.

Spring had sprung and the white of Snowy's show stopper had melted as the north winds blew to and fro like a thief in the night, and age came upon Bianca, but not the manipulability and white magic of the old dwarf witch of the Pacific Northwest, for you see, it was a harsh winter and all she did was to play along so she would have shelter until a much brighter and warmer time came to be so she could sneak away to seek her real treasure of her very own real family; not that of a snow white dwarf witch and so many lost little girls who didn't know how to set themselves free in order to find their way back home.

Now as it so happened one evening, another little girl came upon the cottage of the dwarf witch woman before Bianca escaped a life of slavery. Much to her surprise it was her sister Jezebel.

Well, since no one was aware that twins do exist, especially these two odd ones; all the children and the witch Wanda Wolf who referred to herself so often as Mother Nature wasn't aware Bianca had a look-alike sister, when she knocked on the door to also ask for help in finding her way back home.

The earth had unfrozen itself from the hard winter, birds began to chirp with glee; the girls were all able to go outside once again to be nosy, interfere, snoop and steal as they may as had been directed by Wanda their newly found mother who had cast her evil spell upon them just to benefit her own wicked ego and lust for wealth under the watchful nature of greed and nothing more.

"Who is knocking at my door, I'm coming, hold yourself now, do you hear." She yelled. Wanda had a bad attitude this day and wasn't in any mood to be bothered by anyone since she'd sent all the children out to do her bidding, and in a minute, she had answered the door. "What is it. Who the…? Now didn't I tell you what to do, just turn yourself back around and get busy being my little thief all right Bianca." She said with a wicked tenor to her parched Wiccan voice.

"What do you mean;" said Jezebel; I'm lost, can you help me find my way back home." She began to cry as she spoke giving the old woman her own evil eye in return.

"Girl, don't you talk back to me and give me that look, get your behind in here now before I whip it clean off you." She sounded more like a mean old black leather whips and chains cougar and in a split pea second, she gave Jezebel a yank on her arm pulling her inside even as small as she was.

For you see a dwarf who is a real witch has the strength of ten normal sized women and that is often such a really bad thing, but she didn't know who she was really tangling with and had locked horns at the exact wrong moment and the fight was on.

The old witch hazel was as spry as the spring thaw and had warmed up to the earth where she and her brewed dwell, the tall old tree that was their cottage gave a sinister appearance; giving the impression of being a door, but once inside it was all underground caverns.

The girls had all been turned into small stocky imaginary beings with a bad demeanor in significance of resembling a human; they are associated with mountains, mines, and buried treasures. Dwarves most often have magic powers and can most often be malevolent; and since things had warmed up, they had a break through unto the reality of the upper world coming out to play havoc amongst the normal inhabitants of the whole land of winkin', blinkin', and nod or if you prefer to call it the land of impishness. Yes. Children are this way, that much is known about them out here. My; how naught they were, and when opportunity took its course, one or more of them would cause still other human girls to go and get themselves lost inside the woods where the wild things play, and eventually find their way to the witches cottage to become one of them if they didn't escape through bypassing the bewildered domain of Wanda Wolf the wicked dwarf witch of the Northwest Cascade range of Oregon USA; that by her magic, placed a spell upon the big tree making it appear to be a big cottage in the middle of Nowhere-Ville.

Daylight is not so easily seen when blinded by darkness; there's an overwhelming repression that will flatten anyone who dare try to conquer such an evil dominion so closely connected to the underworld of trickery and the devil' deceit. It will make one null and void if you try to fight her quash with any type of rebellion or political protest completely by any means of force; it is such a quagmire she would lay upon a body when pondering such tactics of the uncanny nature in order to escape her realm of the wickedly cursed in as much as it is to condemn somebody to eternal punishment not being able to see daylight again unless Wanda allowed you to.

Now, Bianca had other plans of the immediate kind and had doubled back so she could sneak by the neurotic overanxious, oversensitive, and obsessive misbehaving about everyday things that most of us won't allow them to be totally fixated and hung-up about inside our rational behavior. Just as she started to pass, she seen what looked like her sister and gave out a hardy shout to run away.

"Jezebel don't go in there, run away as fast as you can, I'm right behind you... she's an evil little woman… RUN." Cried Bianca as she rounded the corner with the speed of the good old gray wolf… Mr. E. H' Wolf who is her mentor here in the world of phantasms wicked this way come narrative.

Getting too close to the wall of the tree cottage, Bianca tore her dress on one of the rickety old door hinges that had come loose during the snow storm a couple weeks before Spring had sprung and began to spread its wild oats all over the land of Un-Enchanted Ville.

Looking at the cottage, she could have sworn that she seen thousands of flakes of gold sparkling in the sun filtered rays that beat their way through the trees in the slight breeze, but she couldn't be for certain; and she latched a hold of Jezebel's hand as she caught up to her fleeing with a gazed look in her pretty sky blue eyes and reddened blackish cheeks.

They ran through the trees as quickly as they could and was soon out of sight of the old dwarf witches hidden cottage inside a huge spruce tree in the forest of Nowhere Ville and Un-Enchanted Ville's dale of the trout.

A dodgy sit on your heels time afterwards the witch made a circular brusque motion with her hands calling for a couple of her hoodwinked children to shadow the two girls before they made their way to the safety zone where none of them could catch them anymore, unless they entered her domain once again; and then, it would be dooms Ville with no such chance of escape what-so-ever in the abrupt future even if it were possible.

Speaking quickly in an unfriendly way using very few words Wanda Wolf dislodged a spell on the forests trees making them to take up root, draw their long tangled and twisted branches into arms in order to help catch Bianca and Jezebel Rose, but it was already too late and she'd lost at least for this time anyway.

Snowy and Etta found a fallen tree passable enough for them to hide in until it was all clear for them to continue back towards where they thought their real home was; the trunk was close by and they heard some movement in side; but they dare not make a whimper and were terse with their whispers back and forth so they wouldn't be discovered and captured by the little evil ones of the wayward and mystifying fractured forest; taken back to the witch where they'd dwell for evermore.

"Shish, don't move or even breathe, I see a shadow coming towards us." Jezebel whispered and then held her breath so it would pass them by.

In an instance their pursuers dissipated clean out of site and Snowy and Etta could breathe and clear their lungs of the rotted trees horrid stench and crawl back out and follow the southern sides of the trees where no moss grows on them and go home at last.

As they stood upright and looked down at the forests floor, they quickly jumped backwards to a brisk movement shuffling its way from beneath the trunks roots; they thought what if it was the old woman crawling her way through underground passages to grab them by the ankles and pull them back down to live a life of sheer misery for all eternity, but at a second glance it was only a couple of squirrel's playing and chasing one another.

All of the sudden the two furry long tail animals turned into two little men with long beards that reached almost to the ground, but before the two girls had a chance to flee, one of the little people's beards got tangled in a briar bush and the other one was working furiously to free his brother elf, but the twisted up one kept flopping around like a fish on dry land while the other one stopped and just kept scratching his head and didn't know what else to do except plea for help with peremptory urgency.

"Beg you I; Help I- he-me brother if can ye female human lass." Cried out the closest one near them, but they were hesitant and just stood there bewildered and couldn't help themselves giggling at the same time.

"I'm sorry but it is funny, Bianca, you go help them, alright my dear sister." Said Jezebel with a smirks grin on her pucker-puss mouth and protruding chin that had slobber drizzling down it like a waterfall. "I can't help it; I am not use to such gaiety the mere jauntiness of such a sight has put me in stitches; make him calm down alright little man with the funny ears… hehehe." Jezebel was beside herself and had to turn her back on all of them as it was her mean nature after all.

"Ah, girls in the meanest human kind, stupid are ye; jollity be it we having till bush it tangled mine brother up. Stand ye there, why? Come ye not give hand unto we two elf, and help it is we give ye in return." Said the little man who had gotten himself caught by the bush that give the impression of being a giant in comparison to him and his brother elf with pointy ears and pee wee style of funny clothing glairing up at Snowy and Etta.

His fire red eyes sneered at the girls as he cried in agony as Bianca walked slowly towards the fairy- imp –pixie- elf with a lingua franca; a form of English that is sometimes used as a way of communicating by people whose first languages are not true English, and that has some of its features that are not usually considered to be correct in real human's standard English.

"Here-here; t-hehe-t-he, little man I will get you out of your mess;" she giggled, "just be still all right or you will make things much worse than they already are. Got it dude." Bianca said with a cheery connotation still laughing; "hehehe," with tears in her bright half red and blue bulging eyeballs and her cheeks of pale blushing pink from watching the little fellow flopping like a fish out of water

"Laugh ye; laugh hardy human girls, funny ye talk; one day time come for ye too." Said both of the pixie-gnome creatures of the forest with a simultaneous - harmonious melody as if they were sparrows that had been grounded from their wings being clipped off.

"Awe how cute; they are trying to sing like birds Snowy, hehehe." Giggled Jezebel in the spirit of the moment as she stood watch in fear of the witch and her own tiny forest goblins what were once real human girls that had gotten lost, captured; and made slaves to a wicked little old woman who dwell in Nowhere Ville just beyond the Columbia Gorge.

"If were it neigh be I tangled here up so, I would make the one of we, but promised me, loosen I and me – Willie, will help ye get back home and out of our sight giant human girl what scare me so, ye do look so alike." Growled the small lively imaginary being what resembled a human with pointed ears, often considered to have a mischievous nature and magical powers that was caught in the bushes by his long gray – twisted curly beard?

"Now hold still, ah this is really caught, Bianca are you still carrying your knife in your pocket?" Bianca said in a mean accent to her real nature.

"Now what ye to do with sharp tool on elf Willie Lingua Franca; hurt me not, or help not I give ye?" Whimpered the funny little creature of the forest as Jezebel handed the knife to Bianca.

"Do you fret me little man, I will not harm you and will only set you free if that is alright with you and your brother?"

Bianca asks as she opened the small but sharp pocket knife with a big smile upon her tiny black and pinkish moist-plump lips.

"Harm me say ye, NOOOOOOO, KEEP WAY YE FROM FACE OF MINE; JUST LEAVE HAIR AND BEARD LONELY… AHHHH!!!" Shouted the elf as loud as he could out of his dreadlocks of anxiety.

"Just shut your mouth little man or we will just go away and leave you here for the forest animals or worse yet that awful dwarf witch Wanda and her crazy wild flower children from Nowhere Ville!" Stated Jezebel with her usual antagonistic accent in spite of her right to just be heard above everyone else.

"Odious ye be, mean ye be milkweed face human girl." Said the one who wasn't twisted in the prickly bramble bush.

"Come on Bianca, let's go, these funny faced little things do not want our help." Demanded Etta as she stuck her tongue out at both of the elves and began to walk away with her nose up in the air like the snobbish little teenage brat that she was in real life beyond her blood curled and sudden transformation of sister to sister.

"NO-OO, HELP WE; ME AND BROTHER MINE, STAY AND FREE I AND HELP YE WE DO." Shouted Willie Franca Lingua who suddenly gave a yank on Jezebel's torn dress causing it to rip all the more.

"Now see what you done to my clothes, you will just have to fix this as well as to help us find our way back home now won't you stupid imp; you are meaner than I am, and that just makes me all the madder and if I were a hatter, I'd squish you like the bug you are right where you and your devilish fairy brother are!" Exclaimed Jezebel as Bianca stood at the ready to hacksaw away at little Willie Lingua Franca's hair and beard.

"Come on Jezzy, you know we need their help as much as they need ours. Right?" Bianca asked her horrid sister and quivered her lower lip just to see if she would laugh just a little bit.

"AHHHH… CUT YE ME PRIDE BAD HUMAN GIRL."
Yelled the pewee elf as he was finally set free; Lingua danced
with joy although he was a bit upset over getting clipped, but
knew that it was necessary.

"There you are little fellow, not it's your turn to help us."
Bianca smiled glancing down at both elves with puppy-dog
eyes.

"Free be I, but help ye we not, now get out of me face mean
human waifs, go on be gone with ye." Said the one who had
stood idly by as the hair cutting was taking place on his
brother. 'Lie we do, fool ye be, not we." He declared; and, in
an instance they were both gone back under the tree trunk
whence they had come from.

"AHHH, THOSE INGRATEFUL LITTLE IMPS, NOW MY
DANDRUF IS UP." Yelled Jezzy as Bianca began to cry.

"Now what are we to do, we will never get out of this
horrible place and back to the safety and warmth of our
cottage." Wept Bianca furiously, but all the sudden out of the

clearing came a big bear growling and snarling for all it was worth.

"Run Etta, it's a mean old black bear." Quenched Jezebel, but Bianca latched onto her dress sleeve before she could flee out of fear of being eaten alive.

The bear paid them no never mind but began to claw at the tree trunk pilfering for tasty morsels. Bianca stood there unafraid as Jezzy took several faced dance paces backwards and fell over a nearby branch; her dress flew up over her head and exposed her behind, the bear turned and walked over towards where she lay as still as the forest floor; it took a big sniff; sneezed a couple times and then went back to digging at the trees trunk.

All the sudden out popped one of the Elf, shaking his fist haphazardly with a frenzied pace and no one could understand what he was saying as his voice was clobbering at a hundred kilometers an hour upon the bears nose or so it seemed, but the bear gave him its evil eye and gobbled him up in one tiny bite and then belched, turned and walked away as if nothing had ever happened what-so-ever.

Poof went a small cloud of bark dust, and out came the other elf also screaming bloody murder as the two girls just laughed at him hysterically.

"Now will you help us find our way back home before I call my bear friend back to eat you too?" Bianca said as Jezzy picked herself up off the ground with tears in her eyes and sweat on her brow.

Jezebel-Briaretta was amazed at what had just transpired before her bulging eyes. She looked at Snowella giving her a quick little smile, but didn't say a solitary word.

Of course the elf was also afraid when Bianca told him she'd call the bear back to eat him equally as well; immediately he agreed to help them get back home, but there was more that they wanted from him and let their wishes be known without hesitation of any kind.

"Go get your bag with all the riches in it that you have stolen from others including the dwarf witch Wanda Wolf and if you don't bring it back in a few minutes, then I will just have to summon back that bear to eat you faster than lightening striking right where you stand. Is that clear little man thing? Now scat little thief and be quick about it, got it?" Bianca demanded and in a flash dance, poof, he was gone beneath the stump, and in another split second, poof, he was back with his bag more than full of riches.

"Here, now ye be gone and me leave alone for all time." Said the Elf still shivering in his tiny black and tan boots with golden trim about them.

"Wait a minute squirrely little fellow, you also promised us that you'd help us get home again and safely now did you not?" Asked Jezebel in her sister's character, while in the process, their personalities seemed to be getting back to their own normality as time passed, but they paid it no never mind and went on about what they had to do in order to get back home where they belonged once and for all.

"Now ye reasonable be to Elf Lingua, me go now… bye-bye." He said in fear that his end may soon come like his brothers had done, but before he had a chance to escape;

both girls snatched him up by his pointy ears making him let

out a high pitched bellow that wasn't so mellow to their ears,

and in a flash, the bear leaped forth before them and gave a

mighty growl and at the ready to gobble that fairy leprechaun

right up for its other snickering snack.

"AHHHH, NO LET BEAST EAT LINGUA, I HELP YE NOW,

MAKE GRIZZLY GO WAY BEG YE SAY I." Shouted that

cowardly small man with magical powers all decked out in

green, who most of the time worked as a shoemaker, knowing

where all treasure is hidden.

The bear knew; and since she couldn't talk in the human

language it just stood their ready for more food, but it just did

not dawn on Bianca and Jezebel that the leprechaun could

make them filthy rich beyond their wildest imagination; and the

Elf now dangled from their fingertips just above the bears

partially open salivating big mouth at an increased rate when

food is seen, smelled, or expected; anticipation was waiting,

and the bear almost raised herself up in order to chew that

thieving spirit up like it was nothing more than a tasty forest

basket full of juicy blackberries.

"NOOOOO, LET NOT IT GET LINGUA." He yelled, and

with a wave of his hand, the two girls vanished before his and

the lady bears eyes, and the Elf fell right into the bear's mouth

and was gone in a jumping jack flash and a bat of a bear's

eye.

Jezebel and Bianca flickered away into thin air as more

than enough gold dust than was in the land of winkin' blinkin'

and nod flew with the wind right after the twin girls straight to

their home much faster than a bolt of lightning.

Well the whole forest echoed with the voice of that Elf

before he went into the bears belly; "'Uncouth human; Lingua

no more be but belly feed for Bear… oh woo was me." He

cried one last tear as the bear walked back to her cave to

check up on her cubs before taking them into the forest to look

for their own food for the very first time in their lives now that

they were old enough to start learning on their own what a

Grizzly Bear eats besides Fairies and other illusory beings just to help out humans also live better lives and learn valuable lessons along the path to happiness and freedom.

"Bianca is that you?" Jezebel said in her own voice, but with a joyous melody like the singing of a meadow Whippoorwill.

"Jezebel is that you." Echoed Bianca in the same melodious squeak, cheep, and meadows call of a chirping Whippoorwill' song.

They gave each other a big hug and began to jump, dance and play in harmony because of sheer delight of being back home once more, or so they thought, but before the Elf died, he sent them back to the lair of Wanda the Dwarf Witch because he knew he was doomed just like his brother had been.

"Ah-ha, now the both of you are here, and here you'll stay forever with no escape. Girls, look who came back, it's your two new sisters, take them to their room, chain and padlock the door tightly now, and soon, they too will be as all of us are, little people… hehehehehe." Wanda said with a cheery tone of voice in her Germanic accent.

"Now what will we do Jezebel, mother must be worried plumb crazy by this time, is there anything we can do to really escape again?" Asked Bianca as she began to cry her eyes out.

"Maybe we can call our friend the bear to help us again?" Jezzy questioned with some tears in her eyes also. "But I don't think she will hear our cry for help way over here do you?" She said as she sat down on the floor with her head between her legs sobbing and slobbering all over the front of her still torn dress.

"Your right my sweet sister, but at least we're together and back to being our own selves again, that's one good thing." Bianca said as she plopped herself down beside her sister also weeping for real, for the very first time in history, like the meadow Whippoorwill losing her precious freedom for all eternity.

Nightfall was upon them and they knew when morning came again, they too would be turned into dwarfs like Wanda and all the other lost children of the wicked witch of the western Oregon coasts Wiccan forest and they were with all of the horrible spiritual practices involving nature-worship and witchcraft that all dwarfs use diligently without any hesitation at every opportunity set before their beady greedy little eyes.

"Biologically the small statured thieving petite, pint sized pixie-goblins in the realm of fantasy land always make everyone else seem unimportant by comparison just like a cathedral' with enormous towering blocks surrounding them; their stocky and pathetic posture is always humped over like old mindless and feeble people with a malevolent growth hormone deficiency with no medical reasons whatsoever to justify their mischievous behavior for such illusory - pretend in-humanoid status quo compared to the rest of the worlds real human beings in outlying areas many kilometers away from this Nowhere Ville near the other dwarf conifer known as Un-Enchanted Ville, Oregon; U S of A!" Explained Jezzy Etta who was much more smarter than her two-minute older sister was.

"We must not allow them to make us like they are, and we must ask our maker to send the bears to help us before it's too late!" Stated Snowy drying her eyes making them like dark chocolate puffed pastry all light and flaky with multilayered and cracked outer shells that had been rolled repeatedly from folding them with her hands that were like extremely rich buttery dough as her essence had swollen and had risen during the baking process of her own misadventure of running away in the first place while eating lots of wild forest foods, but somehow she had went and got heavy with child, but just didn't know she had, and neither did her sister as far as that went.

For the better part of the evening they felt as if their lives were as a lion's share all idiomatic in expression which had developed into a number of fables like that of good old Olivia Phaedrus Library the ancient Greek story-teller who is said to have been a slave to the idiom of the north wind serving up fables to not only little children like they were, but to the Greek Goddess Aphrodite the goddess of love and beauty. She was the daughter of Zeus and as good of an equivalent to the Roman' Venus. They too are only a fairytale and a mythology just to entertain the curiosity for those who believe these fables and myths that belong to a particular people or culture and tell about their ancestors, heroes, gods and other supernatural beings, and history, but we all know they aren't really true… or are they?

We can gain lots of carnal knowledge from these bodies of stories, ideas, and beliefs as folklore, legends, and tradition dictate to our little pointy ears that allow our eyes to see them come to life and drag us into their realm to dwell there permanently like Bianca and Jezebel Rose; that is, unless we escape, go home, and hop into a nice comfy feather-down bed and drift off once again into la-la land where all of our dreams just may be that of reality after all, especially with regard to the lifestyle and attitudes of those living there or associated with it.

Bianca Snowella Rose and her twin sister Jezebel Briaretta Rose are both now little dwarf flowers in Nowhere Ville taking up the hideous and mischievous ways of the Pacific Northwest Oregon's realm of lost children; making havoc while they steal from their counterpart of real life normal humans and luring

other little girls into their new world to dwell as dwarfs for ever

more.

Not The End – YET!

Other books by this extraordinaire author at:

https://www.amazon.com/-/e/B0076PEO2C

Get them before they come get you. HA! HA! HA!

®™ E. Holman II – a Wolf Publisher, Author, Editor, Cover

Designer…

About the Author

Edward Holman II was born in Muncie, Indiana in 1950.

Along the road to achieving his goal of becoming an author,

he had a hard life with many twists and turns along the way.

He resides in the Great Pacific Northwest in Portland, Oregon,

USA. He has 5 children all adults and on their own. He

continues to always strive forward as a domesticated

household technician in spite of the many obstacles along

life's narrow path.

Although he has been divorced twice, and been single

since 2009, he is hopeful to find his last love at age 69. I ask.

If, you be a real woman, not pretentious, and be between 50

and 60, ht., wt. proportionate, and a caregiving type of woman and seeking your last love as well. Make first contact. Will ye? 'Tis no fantasy my dear.

Ed is always skillfully crafting his novel works of literary genre with innovative, provocative, controversial, and unusual proficiency inside the world of literature. So with this said about Edward Holman II, enjoy this - your imaginary journey like he does on a daily basis.

God bless, Thank you my fairytale creatures divine.

Edward Holman II